AT THE
BEACH

by Melanie Hope Greenberg

E. P. DUTTON   NEW YORK

Dedicated to the child spirit in everyone.

Special thanks to
Jane, Lucia, and Bob & Barbara T.

Published in the United States by
E. P. Dutton, New York, N.Y.,
a division of NAL Penguin Inc.
Published simultaneously in Canada by
Fitzhenry & Whiteside Limited, Toronto
Designer: Barbara Powderly
Printed in Hong Kong by South China Printing Co.
First Edition   10 9 8 7 6 5 4 3 2 1

Library of Congress Cataloging-in-Publication Data
Greenberg, Melanie Hope.
   At the beach/by Melanie Hope Greenberg.—1st ed.
      p.   cm.
   Summary: Evokes the mood prevailing at the beach where the sun
shines, seashells whisper, waves froth, and sand castles grow tall.
   ISBN 0-525-44474-2
   [1. Beaches—Fiction.]   I. Title.   88-29995
PZ7.G82755At   1989   CIP
[E]—dc19   AC

At the beach
surrounded by sunshine

toes squish in hot grainy sand
where starfish snuggle

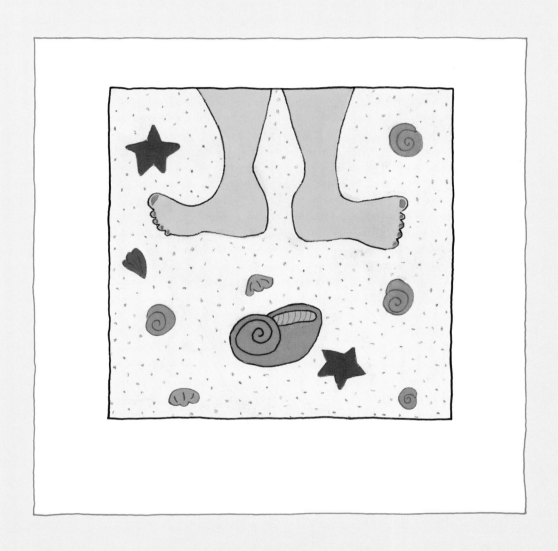

and seashells whisper
sounds of waves
breaking on land far away.

A sea gull swoops
to catch his slippery meal
and a kite climbs upward
to the clouds

while high in the sky
an airplane flies,
with flapping banners behind.

At the beach
a sand castle grows tall,
sprinkled with rocks and shells.
A flag on the tower
beckons sea gulls to sit
on ledges

and eat bread crumbs
from waiting hands.

At the beach
waves froth and foam
on sandy feet

and gently rock a fat sea horse
out where the silver fish
jump and dive.

At the beach
towels rub off sand and sea,

sleepy heads rest
on sun-warmed blankets

and sea gulls gather noisily
to say good-bye.